♡ Eva in the Spotlight ♡

Read more OWL DIARIES books!

OWL DIARIES

♡ Eva in the Spotlight ♡

Rebecca Elliott

BRANCHES™

SCHOLASTIC INC.

For the Peacock family,
my flap-tastic feathery friends who
are always up for a party. — R.E.

Library of Congress Cataloging-in-Publication Data

Names: Elliott, Rebecca, author. | Elliott, Rebecca. Owl diaries ; 13.
Title: Eva in the spotlight / Rebecca Elliott.
Description: First edition. | New York : Branches/Scholastic, 2020. |
Series: Owl diaries ; 13 | Summary: Eva's class is putting on a play,
Snowy White and the Seven Owlets, but Eva is a little disappointed
when she is cast as the Magic Mirror (and Snowy White's understudy);
the owl students are making all the sets, props, and costumes,
and rehearsal is a little chaotic—but the play is going well until
Snowy White hurts her leg and Eva has to fill in for real.

Identifiers: LCCN 2019052815 | ISBN 9781338298758 (paperback) |
ISBN 9781338298765 (library binding) | ISBN 9781338298789 (ebk)
Subjects: LCSH: Owls—Juvenile fiction. | Children's plays—Juvenile
fiction. | Elementary schools—Juvenile fiction. | Diaries—Juvenile
fiction. | Snow White (Tale)—Drama—Juvenile fiction. | CYAC:
Owls—Fiction. | Theater—Fiction. | Schools—Fiction. |
Diaries—Fiction.
Classification: LCC PZ7.E45812 Eq 2020 | DDC [Fic]—dc23
LC record available at https://lccn.loc.gov/2019052815

10 9 8 7 6 5 4 3 2 1   20 21 22 23 24

Printed in China   62
First edition, August 2020

Edited by Katie Carella
Book design by Maria Mercado

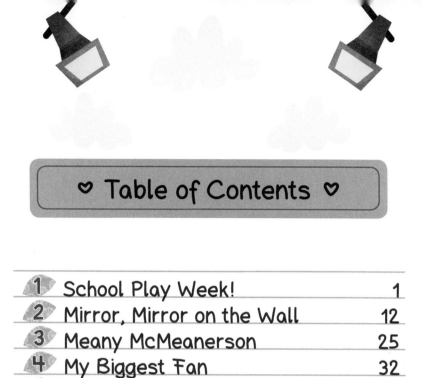

♡ Table of Contents ♡

♡ School Play Week! ♡

Sunday

Hi Diary,

It's Eva Wingdale again. I'm just **FLAPPING** with excitement because this week is SCHOOL PLAY week! I can't wait to tell you about it! But first, here's a bit about me . . .

<u>I love</u>:

Moonlight
flights

When Granny
Owlberta makes
me giggle

Hanging with
my friends

New pajamas

Acting!

Singing!

Wearing costumes

The word clap

I DO NOT love:

Foggy
nights

WAA WAA!

Anyone in my family
feeling sad

Falling off
trees

WHOOPS!

Spilling stuff on
my pajamas

Boo!

Forgetting my lines

Holes in my favorite shoes

Costume problems

The word <u>stink</u>

STINK

This is my **FLAPTASTIC** family.

Dad

Mom

Humphrey

Happy Birthday, Granny Owlberta!

Granny Owlberta

Me

Baby Mo

Grandpa Owlfred

This is my pet bat, Baxter.

He's THE BEST!

I'm super happy that I am an owl.

We can look
behind us without
turning our bodies.

We're awake all night long.

We fly super fast.

WHOOSH!

Our feathers are soft and good for cuddles.

I live in
a blue tree
house on
Woodpine
Avenue in
Treetopolis.

11

My BFF Lucy
lives in the orange
tree house next door.

9

My school is called Treetop Owlementary. Here is a photo of my class:

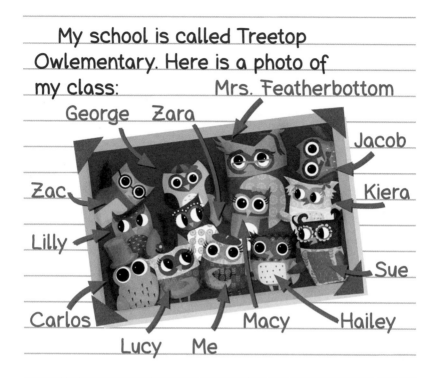

George Zara Mrs. Featherbottom
Jacob
Zac Kiera
Lilly
Sue
Carlos Macy Hailey
Lucy Me

I'm so **EGG-CITED** about school tomorrow! Mrs. Featherbottom is going to tell us which play our class is doing. I can't WAIT to find out!

♡ Mirror, Mirror on the Wall ♡

Monday

Tonight, Granny Owlberta came over for breakfast. She looked a bit sad. You see, Grandpa Owlfred is away all week. (He's building new tree houses on the other side of the forest!)

I told Granny about the school play and that cheered her up.

Diary, I hope I get the starring role in the play. That would REALLY make Granny smile!

When I got to school, everyone was **HOOTING** about what our class play might be.

14

We all held our breath as
Mrs. Featherbottom started talking.

As you all know, we will be performing a play this Friday. You will each have an acting role <u>and</u> a job to do on set. And the play will be . . .

There's SO much to do! This is the list we came up with:

- Write the script

- Design the set

- Build the set

- Learn our lines

- Practice the songs

- Learn the dance moves

- Make the costumes

- Design the programs

At the end of the night,
Mrs. Featherbottom posted our parts
in the play and our jobs offstage, too.
We crowded around to see the list.

CAST LIST

Mrs. Featherbottom: director
Sue: Snowy White & director's assistant
Carlos: Evil Queen & head of props
Zac: Prince & script writer
Kiera: Hooty Owlet & script writer
Lucy: Hungry Owlet & costume designer
Macy: Shorty Owlet & set designer
Jacob: Flappy Owlet & lighting designer
Zara: Merry Owlet & program designer
Lilly: Snoozy Owlet & dance choreographer
George: Gloomy Owlet & set builder
Hailey: Huntsman & set builder
Eva: Magic Mirror (and the Snowy White
    understudy) & costume designer

Lucy was right. Even though I had
been hoping to tell Granny Owlberta
that I had the starring role, the play will
be fun no matter what role I have. And
costume design will be fun, too!

After school, I went to visit Granny. She still looked a bit sad without Grandpa, but she perked up when she asked me about the play.

I didn't want to let Granny down, and I am the understudy for the starring role. So it wasn't <u>exactly</u> a lie when I said –

Oh dear, Diary. I can hardly sleep. What am I going to do when Granny comes to see me star in the play? She won't even see me onstage because I'm just the voice of a mirror!

All I'd wanted to do was cheer Granny up. But this was not my best idea.

3

♡ Meany McMeanerson ♡

Tuesday

Tonight we started work on the play.

Carlos made props.

Zac and Kiera wrote the script.

Zara designed the program.

Lilly planned our dance moves.

Macy designed the set.

George and Hailey started building
the set. Jacob set up the stage lighting.

Work faster!
No breaks!

And Sue made sure
we were all doing our
jobs. (Actually, Sue
was being a bit of a
Meany McMeanerson.)

MEANY
McMEANERSON
100555

Although I was still worried about what I had told Granny, Lucy and I had fun making costumes together.

I'm excited to be an owlet! Are you looking forward to being the Magic Mirror, Eva?

I am. I guess I just still sort of wish I was Snowy White.

Just at that moment, Sue flew past and heard what we were saying. Why does she always do that at the wrong time?!

I know Sue doesn't mean to be mean. But that did seem like a pretty mean thing to say.

And it made me feel worse about what I'd said to Granny Owlberta because Sue is right. She is much better at speaking in public than I am. She is the better owl for the job.

At bedtime, I was learning all the Magic Mirror and Snowy White lines when Mom came in. I told her everything.

I didn't get the starring role. I'm just the mirror. But I told Granny I was Snowy White. I lied to cheer her up. And now I feel so bad about it.

Oh, darling. You might have done the wrong thing, but you did it for the right reasons. That being said, you <u>do</u> need to tell Granny the truth before Friday.

I'll tell Granny after school tomorrow.

Don't worry. I'm sure she'll understand. And you're going to shine as the mirror!

Chatting with Mom always makes me feel better. And I know she's right. Granny won't mind that I'm not the star. But I'm still not looking forward to telling her.

♡ My Biggest Fan ♡

Wednesday

I still felt nervous about talking with Granny after school, but rehearsing for the play was so much **FEATHER-FLAPPING** fun!

When we practiced singing and dancing, everyone kept tripping over one another. We were laughing so hard, some feathers fell out!

Carlos tried on the outfit Lucy and I had made for him. We'd sewn the sleeves in the wrong place. He looked SO FUNNY!

How do I look?

Well, it's lucky the Evil Queen is not supposed to be the fairest of them all!

Then Mrs. Featherbottom reminded us that tomorrow would be our dress rehearsal.

Get a good day's sleep today! Tomorrow is our official practice run before the big night!

After school, I flew to Granny's house. I was so nervous about telling her the truth.

Granny, I have to tell you something. I'm sorry, but . . .

Yes, dear?

I'm not going to be Snowy White in the play. I'm just the understudy. I'm really going to be a mirror.

Granny looked so sad. I felt **OWLFUL**.

She tickled me and we both started laughing!

TICKLE! TICKLE!

Thanks, Granny. I'd only told you I was Snowy White because I'd wanted to cheer you up while Grandpa is away.

Oh, I'm fine! It's just a shame Grandpa will miss your show. He won't be home until Saturday.

When I got home, Lucy came over to finish making costumes. I tried on the Snowy White costume so Lucy could put the finishing touches on it.

This costume is so cool! Great work, Lucy!

Thank you! You look <u>flapperrific</u> in it. It's too bad you won't get to be Snowy White when you've learned the lines and everything.

That's okay. We'll all have fun up onstage, right?

Right!

Only two days until the actual show!

The truth is, Diary, while I am still a tiny, little bit sad I won't get to be Snowy White, I'm going to be a **FLAPTASTIC** Magic Mirror! That is, as long as I get all my lines right and remember all my dance moves... EEK!

5

♡ Drama Disaster! ♡

Thursday

Our dress rehearsal started off great tonight! Everyone was in their costumes, and the stage set looked **OWLSOME**.

I am the EVIL QUEEN! Where's my magic mirror?

40

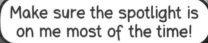

Make sure the spotlight is on me most of the time!

Then it all started to go very, VERY wrong!

Parts of the set kept falling down.

Mirror, mirror on the . . . um . . . floor?

Some costumes didn't fit quite right.

I can't move my wings!

I think my hat's a bit too big!

The stage lights kept flashing so we couldn't see well and kept bumping into one another!

Ooof!

Ooof!

Ooof!

Also, everyone kept forgetting their lines. Especially Sue. Whenever it was her turn to speak, she just stood there going red in the cheeks — until I told her what to say!

The dress rehearsal was a disaster!
Now we were all super worried about
tomorrow.

Well, class, just remember that tomorrow's performance can't possibly go as badly as tonight's. But please practice, practice, practice!
You all need to work MUCH HARDER!

As we worked more on the play, Mrs. Featherbottom put her wing around Sue.

Sue, I think maybe you could spend some more time working on your lines and a bit less time worrying about what everyone else is doing.

Everyone practiced their lines. But I noticed Sue sitting on her own looking down in the dumps.

I felt bad for Sue. I think maybe she spent the week <u>so</u> focused on everyone else that she didn't think about her starring role. Now she's realized she is super nervous about it!

As your understudy, I've learned all your lines, too. So maybe I could help you practice?

Well, I'm sure I <u>could</u> learn them on my own . . . But yes, that would actually be great. Thanks, Eva.

After school, Sue and I flew to her tree house. We went through the Snowy White lines together. I was a bit worried she might be mean and shout-y, but we actually had fun!

Oh, how I love my new friends, the seven owlets: Snoozy, Hooty, Gloomy . . . um . . .

Yes! Keep going!

Dumpy, Cheesy, Stinky and . . . Steve?

Almost!!

I'm glad I helped Sue. Now I can't wait for tomorrow! And — even if the play is a disaster — I know we will all have fun! And I'm excited Granny will be there!

♡ The Show Must Go On! ♡

Friday

It's the night of the show! We put on our costumes while our families took their seats.

It feels like butterflies are doing somersaults in my tummy!

Me too!

And me!

Then Hailey saw that Lilly looked VERY scared.

What's the matter, Lilly?

My whole family is here.
I just don't want to mess
up and let them down.

I know how you feel. My granny has been feeling down, and I REALLY want to do a good job to make her smile.
Come on, Lilly. I'll help you with your costume.
We'll all be great. I just know we will!

It was show time at last. Everything was going great! Well, almost everything...

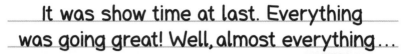

Mirror, mirror, on the wall, who is the —

RIP!

HAHA

Um, most naked of them all!?

HAHA!
HAHA!
HAHA!
HAHA!
HAHA!
HAHA!

The Evil Queen's dress came off! But Carlos loved that it made the audience laugh!

The play quickly got back on track.

But then
halfway through –

DISASTER!

Sue tripped over the curtain and hurt her leg!

I was nervous but also excited. I knew the show had to go on! So, with shaky wings, I put on the costume and became Snowy White!

I flew out onstage.

With the spotlight on me, the audience was very dark. But I could just make out my family. When I saw their proud faces, I knew I could do this!

It was YOU who poisoned me, Evil Queen!

When the play finished, the audience stood up and clapped. I felt **OWLMAZING**!

CLAP!

CLAP!

CLAP!

CLAP!

CLAP!

CLAP!

CLAP!

CLAP!

CLAP!

CLAP!

CLAP!

CLAP!

Then we had a group hug backstage.

Get back out there for one last bow!

Back onstage, Hailey gave
Mrs. Featherbottom flowers.

These are from all
of us. Thank you for
helping us do this!

Oh,
thank
you!

Audience, I am so proud of all the hard
work your little owls put into this flaptastic
play. Let's give them one last cheer!

Everyone **HOOTED** loudly. As Sue and
I walked to the front of the stage for our
final bow, I noticed her leg was better!

Had Sue lied about her leg to get offstage earlier? Was it because she was nervous? Or had she forgotten her lines again? Backstage, I asked Sue about her leg.

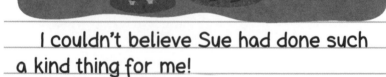

Sue! Your leg is okay!

Oh, yes. I, well … actually I didn't hurt it. I just thought you should do the second half of the play after you learned the lines so well and helped me with mine.

I couldn't believe Sue had done such a kind thing for me!

Thank you, Sue. That was super lovely of you.

Well, I am very lovely.

Then Mom found me backstage.

I looked over and guess who I saw!

Grandpa Owlfred!

Grandpa, I can't believe you're here!

I came home early just to see your play! I arrived halfway through and stood at the back. But I saw your whole performance as Snowy White!

My family all hugged me and said how great the play was.

♡ Eva the Superstar ♡

Saturday

I am sooooo tired, Diary! We had an aftershow party, where we ate toffee apples and danced the day away!

70

Being a superstar is hard work, Diary. But it's really so much fun when you've got **OWLMAZING** friends and family around!

See you next time!